This book belongs to:

....

....

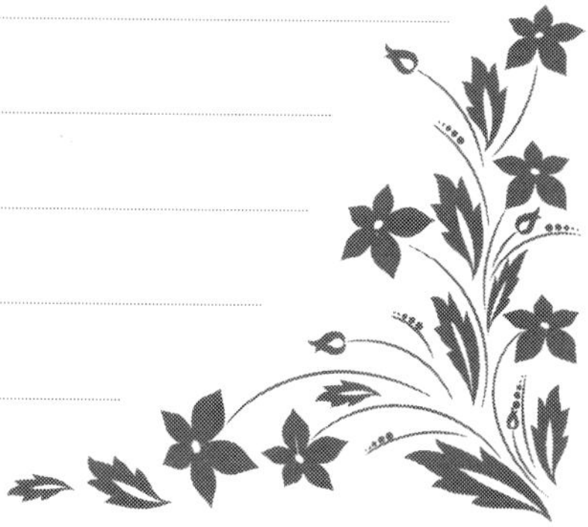

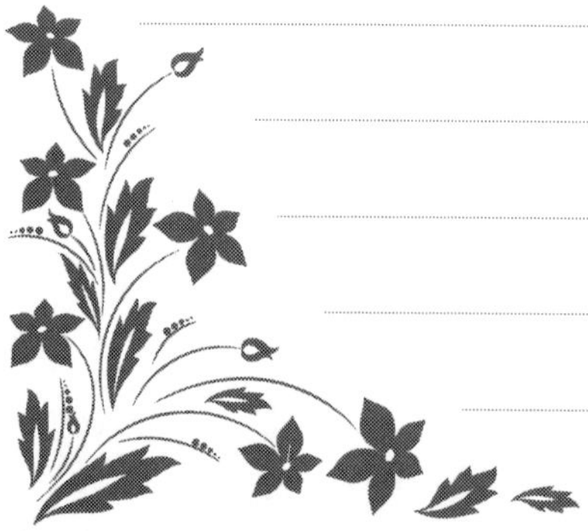

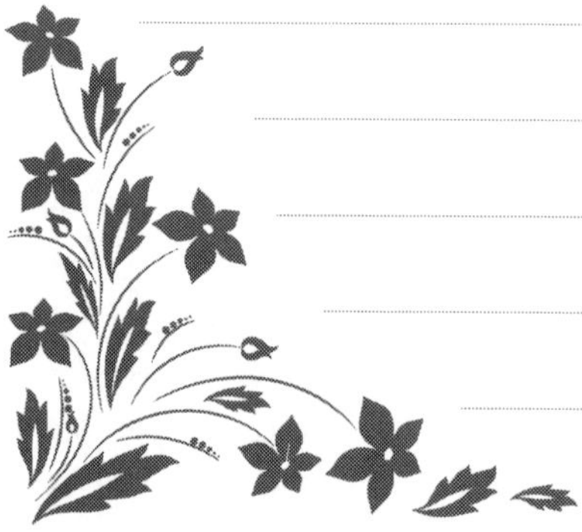

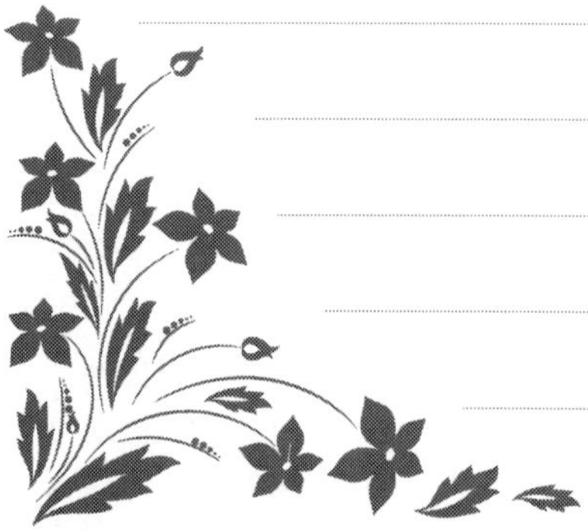

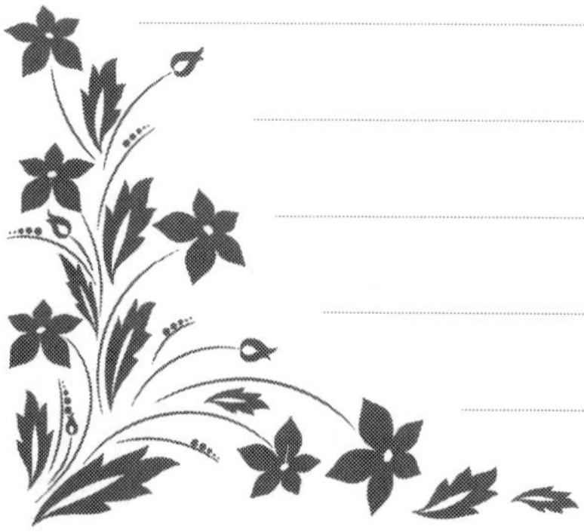

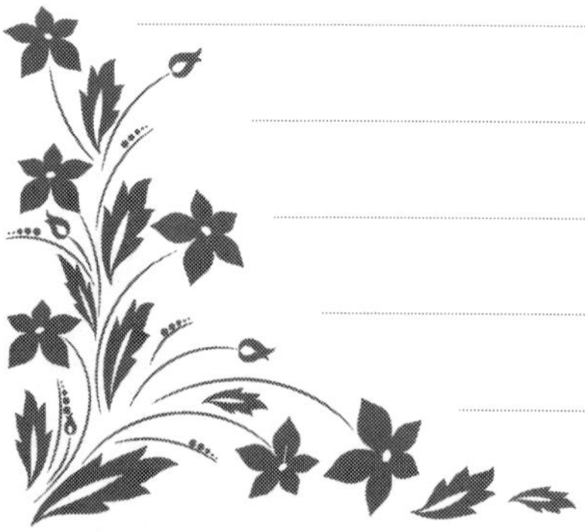

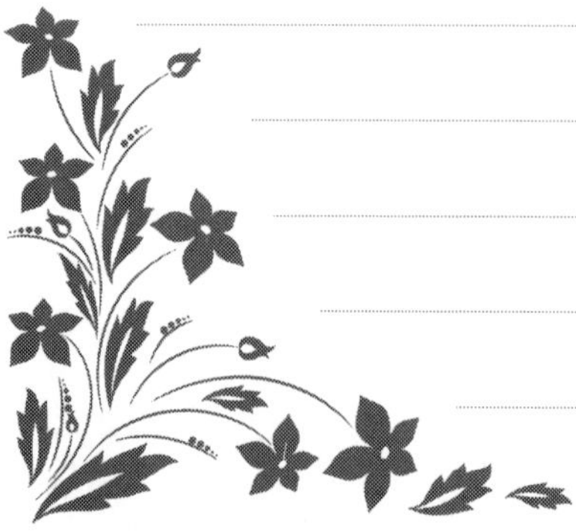

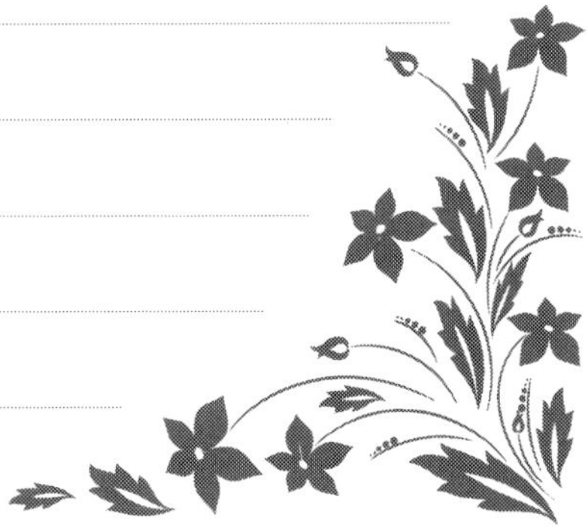

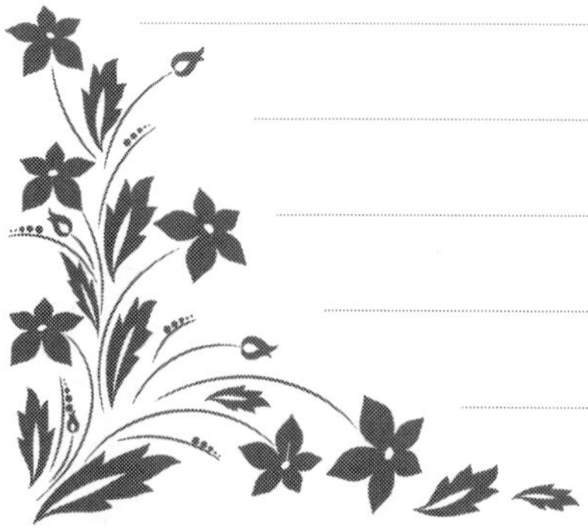

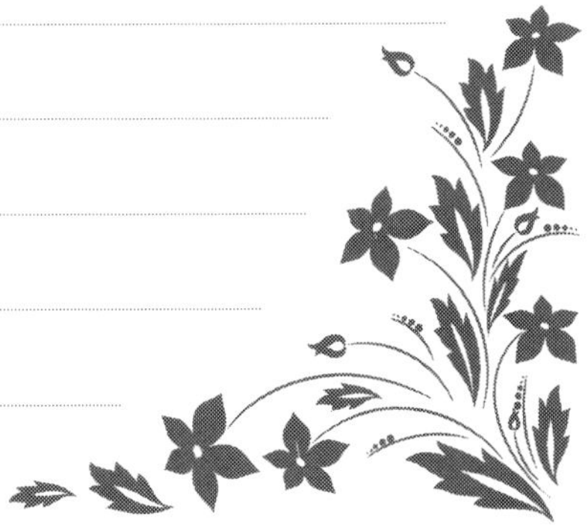

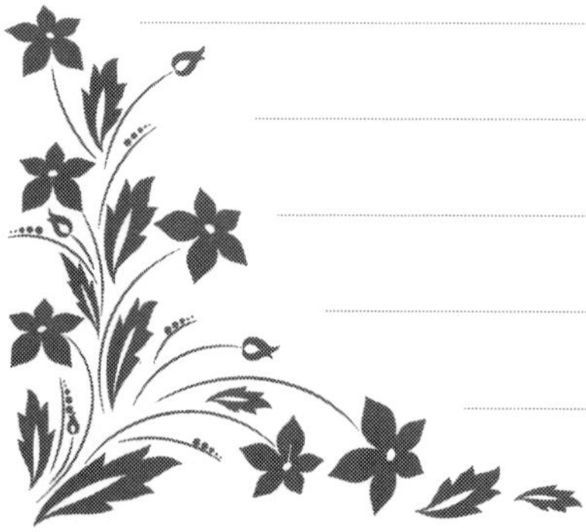

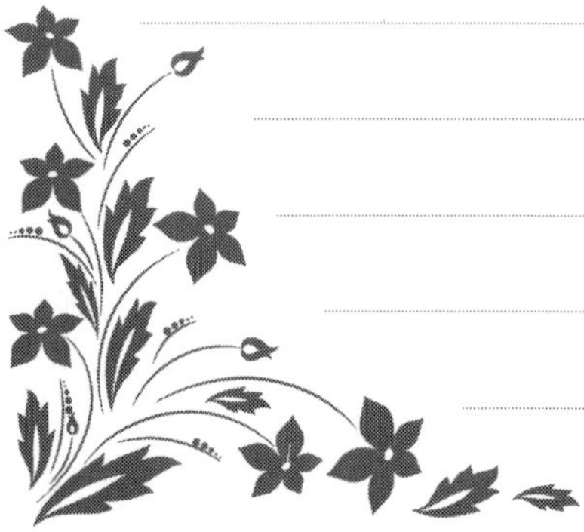

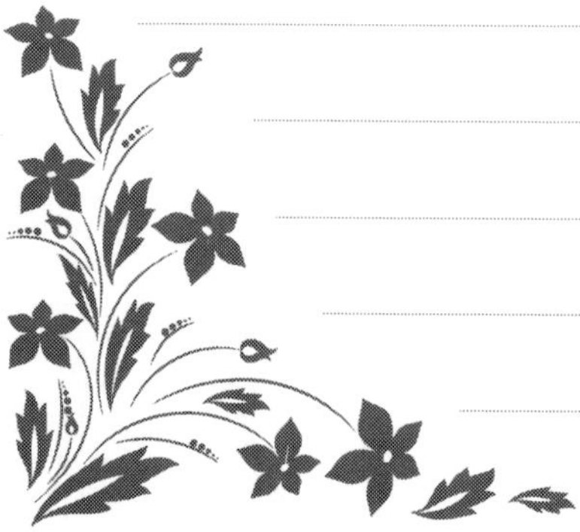

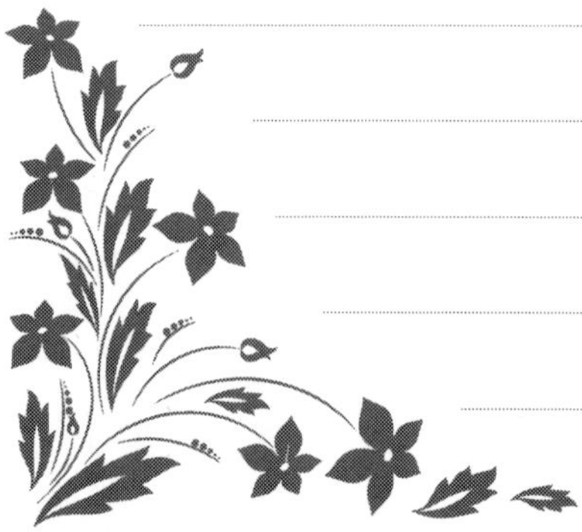

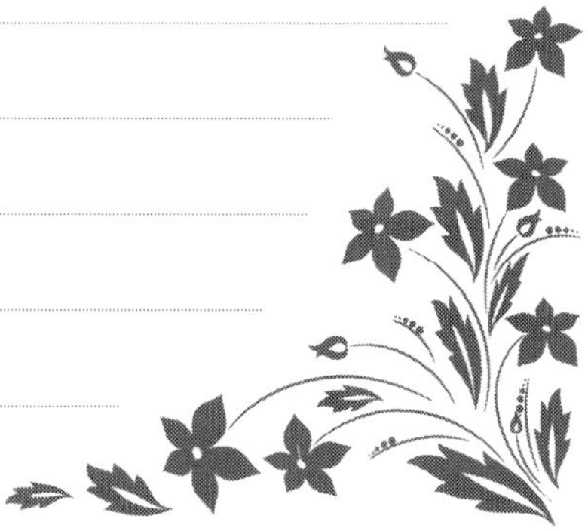

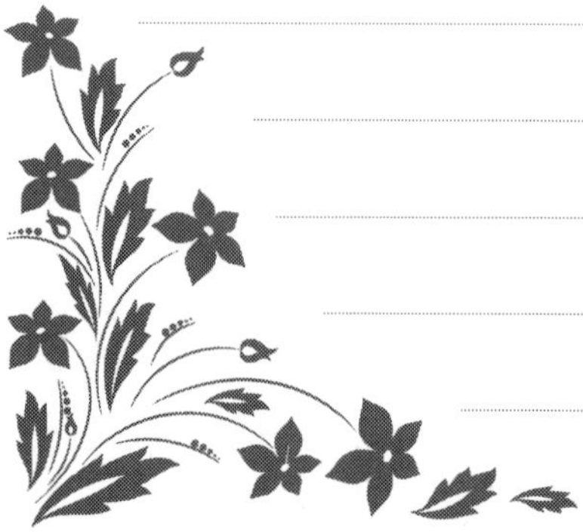

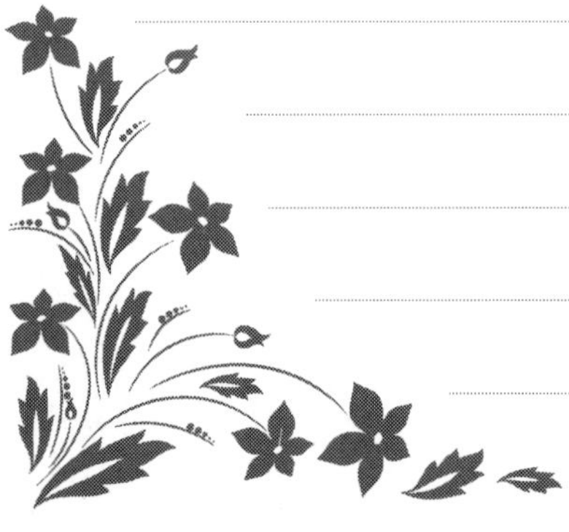

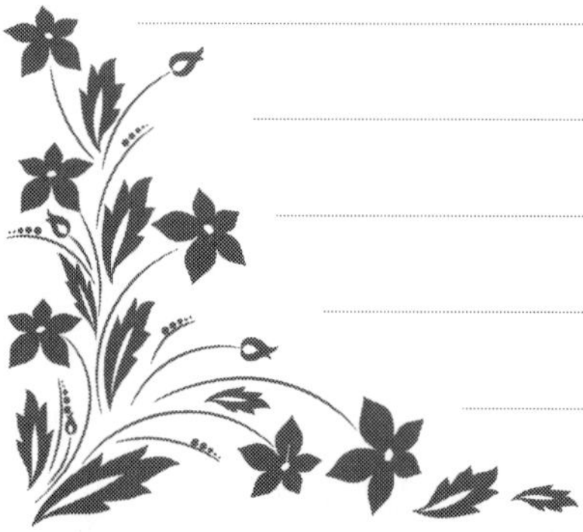

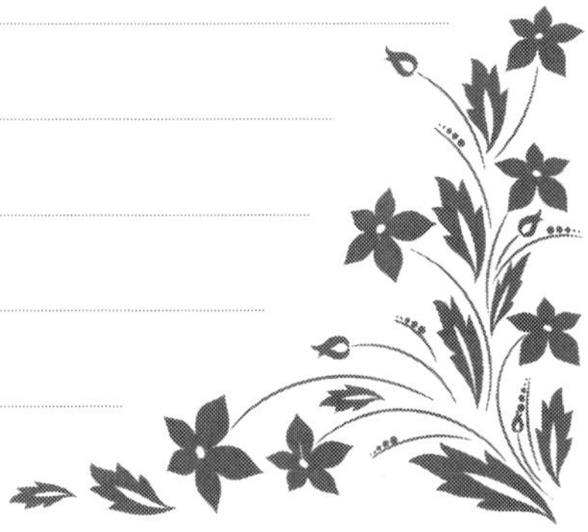

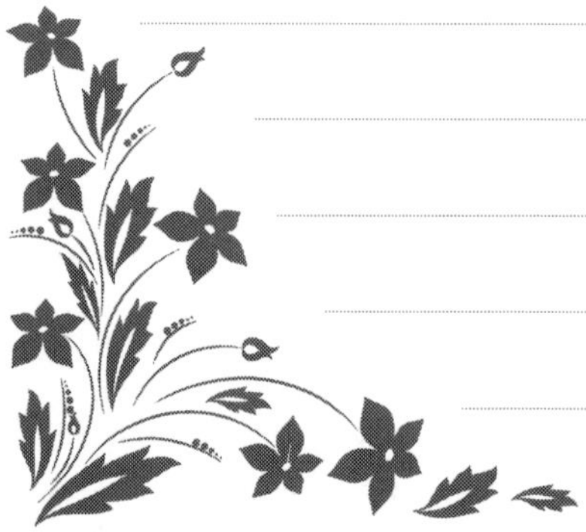

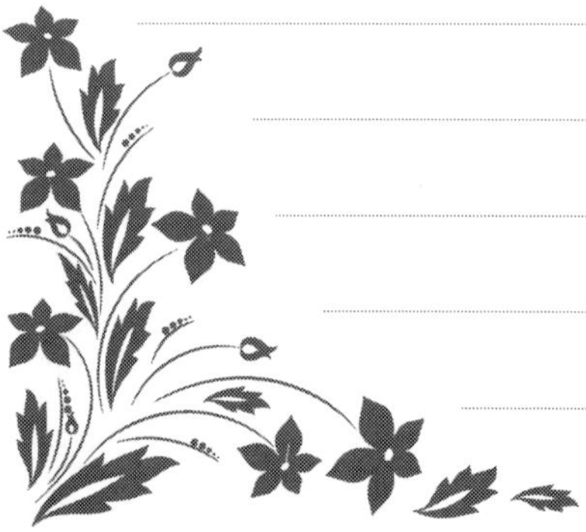

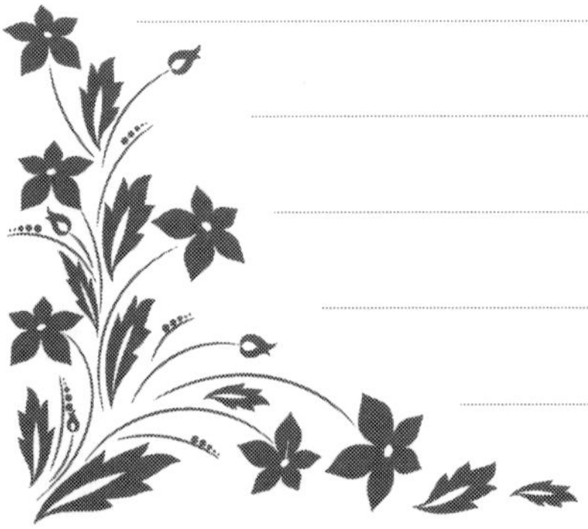

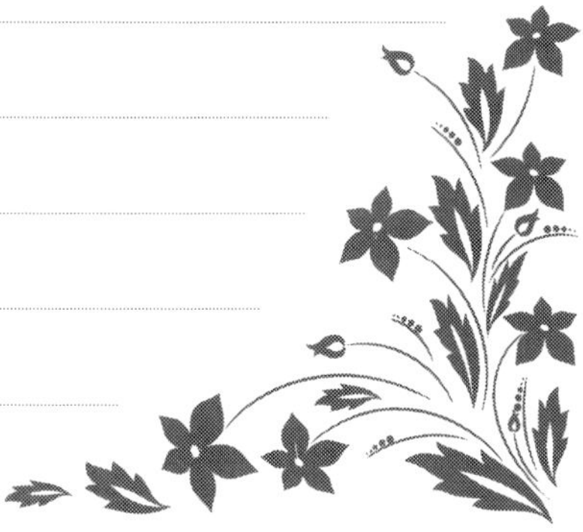

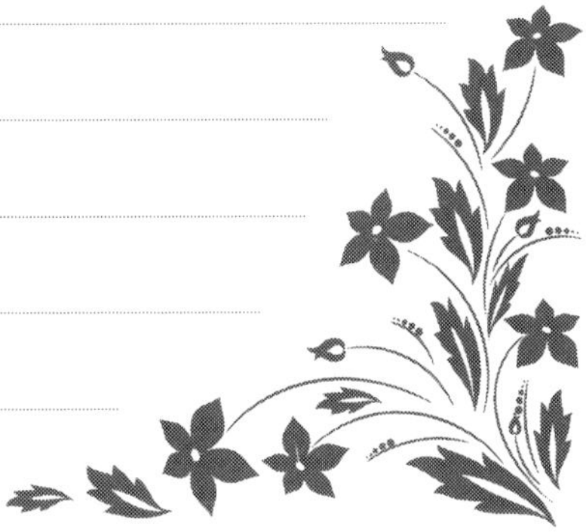

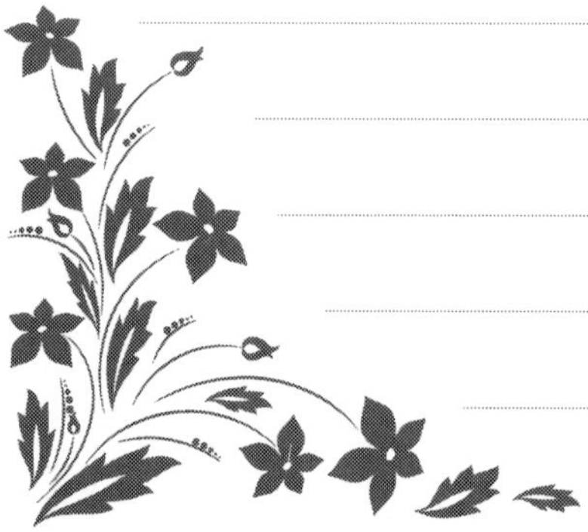

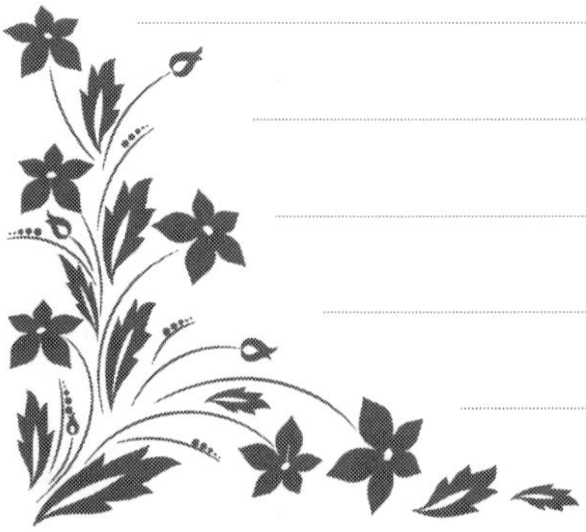

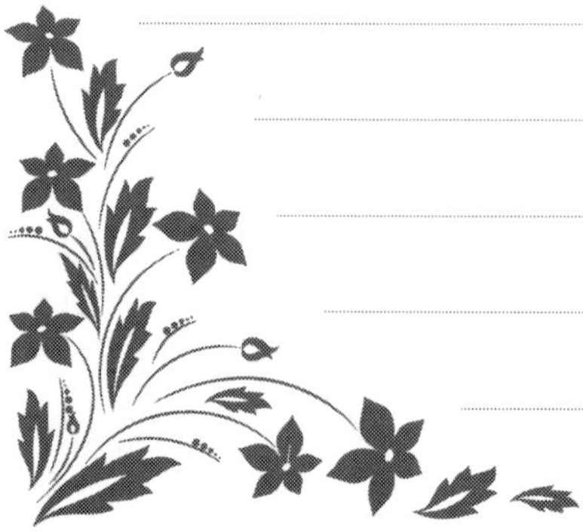

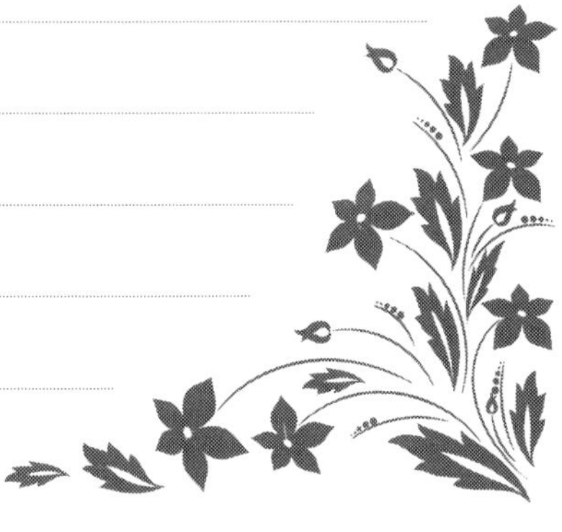

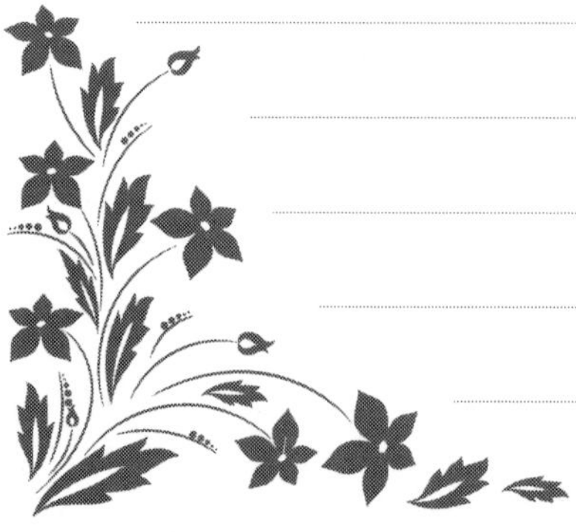

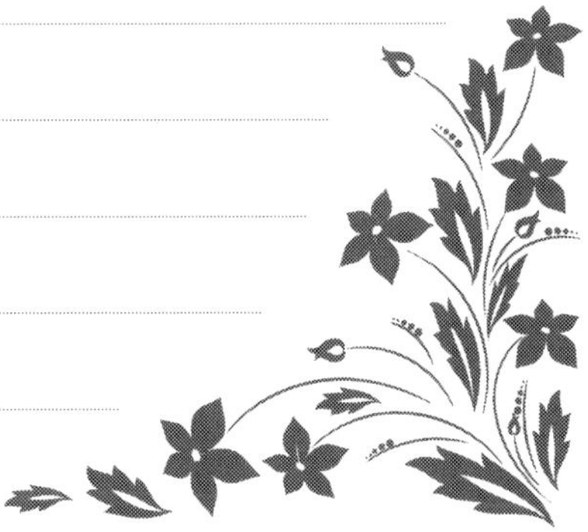

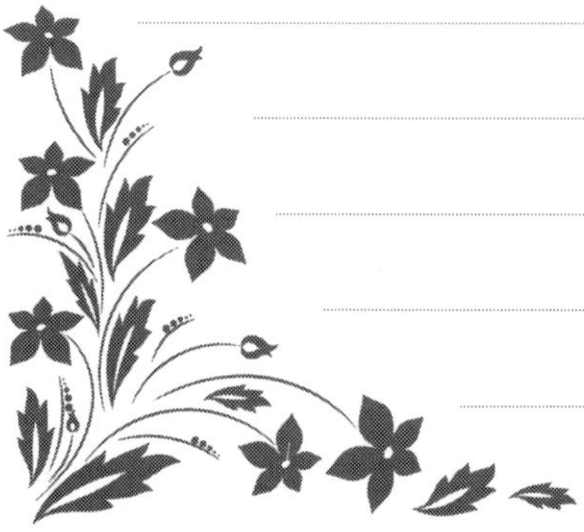

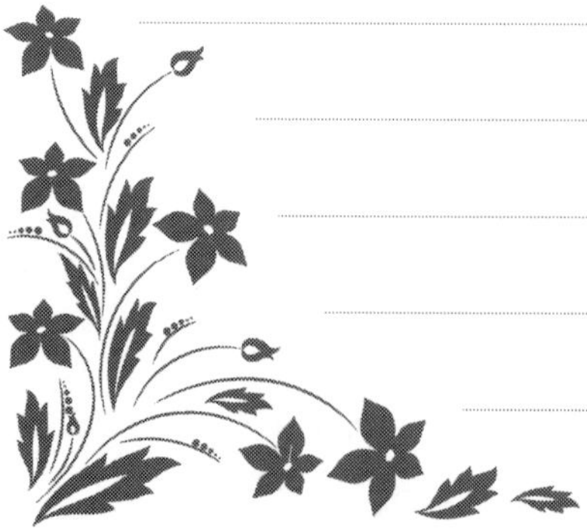

Made in United States
Orlando, FL
05 February 2022

14503849R00067